Blob-farley

Created by Christy Johns
Written & Illustrated by Tim Gagnon

AuthorHouse™
1663 Liberty Drive
Bloomington, IN 47403
www.authorhouse.com
Phone: 1 (800) 839-8640

Published by AuthorHouse

ISBN: 978-1-5462-3074-8 (sc)
ISBN: 978-1-5462-3076-2 (hc)
ISBN: 978-1-5462-3075-5 (e)

Print information available on the last page.

Revision Date: 2/27/2018

authorHOUSE®

Deep in the deepest sea,
lives a dear little fish named **Blob Farley**.

As his name would suggest, Blob Farley is a Blob Fish, and yes,
Blobfish are very real indeed! Living in the ocean depths, Blob
has many friends, like Jill the Jellyfish, Dorothy the Dumbo
Octopus, Leonard the Lantern Fish and so many more.

Yet Blob yearned for something more! For travel, adventure, and most of all, to go to the surface and meet the most fascinating creatures of all! People!

And so saying goodbye to his friends and family, Blob Farley embarked upon his great adventure.

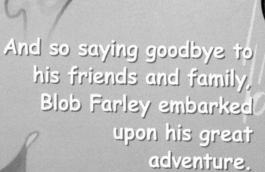

As he rose up from the deep dark sea bottom floor and into the vast blue ocean, he saw a figure approaching from the distance.

Once, twice, three times it circled him.
It was big and long and blue.
With great flashing teeth and a voice as deep as the ocean itself, it said...

"Fancy meeting you here!"

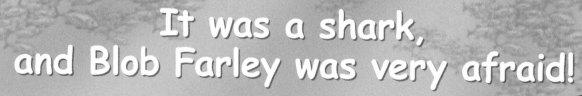

It was a shark, and Blob Farley was very afraid!

But then Blob Farley remembered what his dear mother used to say, "To have a friend, you need to be a friend!", and so, swallowing his fear, Blob Farley introduced himself.

Simon the shark,

with a tear in his eye,
smiled wide and said,
"No fish of the sea has ever not been afraid of me!
It is hard to make friends with a smile like mine!
You are not afraid! You are kind!
You shall have a friend in me!

Simon listened as Blob
told him of his adventure
and decided to help! "Travel up the
water just a bit more and you will
meet someone who can help
you on your way!
Her name is Tina!

Up, up, up, and even further up, Blob swam, until finally, he heard someone singing. Swimming towards the sound he saw the strangest creature he has ever seen.

She had a shell like a giant crab, four flippers and instead of a mouth, it had a beak! When the creature realized that Blob was watching, she swam up to meet him. With a laugh that warmed up the sea, she introduced herself with overwhelming glee!

"Well hello my dear, and who might you be?
Tina the Turtle knows just about everyone
in this vast blue sea, but she doesn't recall
ever meeting thee!"

Blob had never met anyone or anything quite like Tina!
Her smile was wide and she laughed out loud!
She grabbed Blob's fins and made him dance around!

Although a bit overwhelmed, Blob Farley remembered what his mother used to say. **"To have a friend you need to be a friend."** And so with a gulp, he introduced himself.

Tina and Blob talked and talked and talked.
Then, they sang and sang and sang some more.
And then, they danced! After all that...
Tina offered to help!

"Travel up just a bit further
and you will reach the surface.

Look for
Donald
and
Daisy
the
Dolphins
and be sure to
tell him that Tina
sent you!
They will be happy

to show you the
rest of the way!

And so Blob Farley said farewell to Tina the Turtle and traveled further up. Up, up, up he swam and it wasn't soon before he saw the sun sparkling through the top of the water!

The surface! He made it! From the bottom to the top! But where were the Dolphins?

Suddenly, Blob heard a great big splash! And then another! Turning around to see what it was, Blob Farley found himself face to face with two of the oddest creatures he had ever met!

"Hi there little fellah! What brings you here? My name is Donald and this is Daisy! We are dolphins!"

Blob explained his adventures to Donald and Daisy. How he left the depths of the sea and how he met Simon and Tina and most of all, his quest to meet people just like you and just like me.

Donald and Daisy, were as glad as could be, "Come with us Blob Farley! We'll show you the way!

All the way to the Shoreline where the people play!

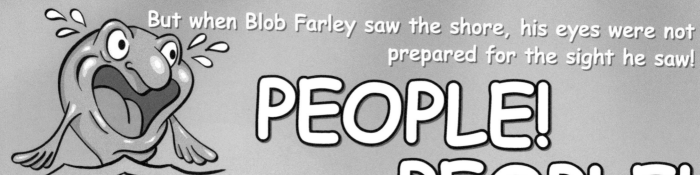

But when Blob Farley saw the shore, his eyes were not prepared for the sight he saw!

PEOPLE! PEOPLE!

Swallowing his fear, Blob swam for the shore, and to his surprise, the children were ecstatic to see such a sight! What a wondrous fish, said one to another, what could it be? It's like nothing we've ever seen! Blob explained that he was a Blobfish, from deep in the depths, that he was made of jelly, and nothing else!

The children were amazed and laughed with delight,
and Blob Farley played with them...
straight through till night!

Blob Farley's adventure was a great one indeed,
he had made new friends and done amazing things.
Now he had to go back to the deep, deep sea,
but he told the children he would be back,
just you see!

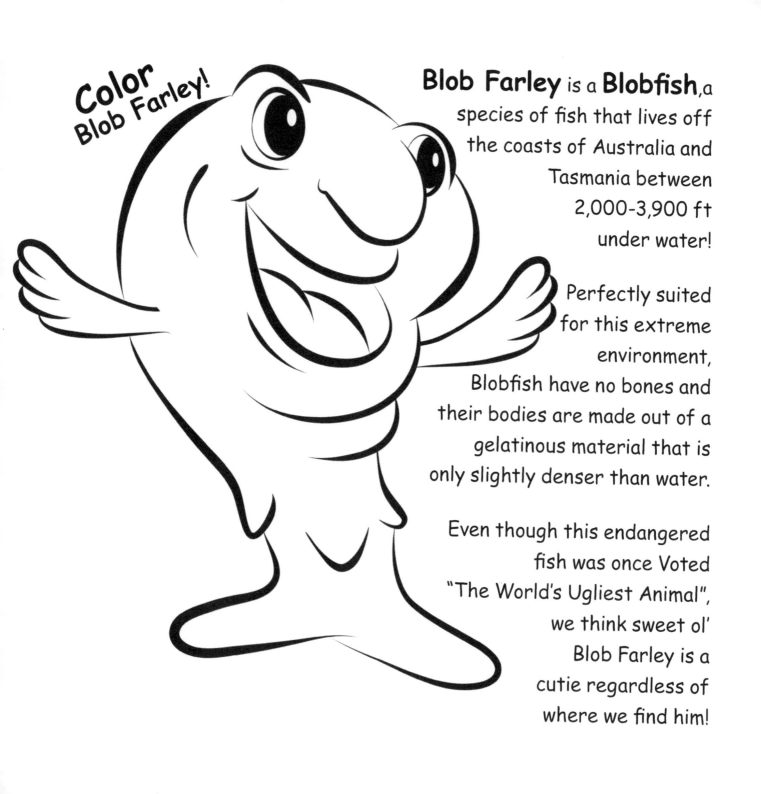

Color Blob Farley!

Blob Farley is a **Blobfish,** a species of fish that lives off the coasts of Australia and Tasmania between 2,000-3,900 ft under water!

Perfectly suited for this extreme environment, Blobfish have no bones and their bodies are made out of a gelatinous material that is only slightly denser than water.

Even though this endangered fish was once Voted "The World's Ugliest Animal", we think sweet ol' Blob Farley is a cutie regardless of where we find him!

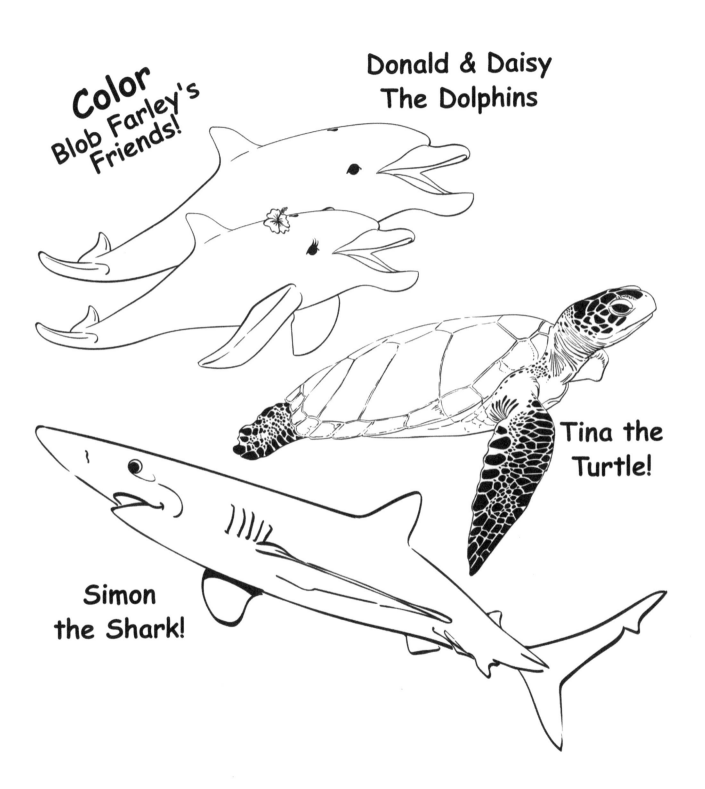

Color Blob Farley's Friends!

Donald & Daisy The Dolphins

Tina the Turtle!

Simon the Shark!

CPSIA information can be obtained
at www.ICGtesting.com
Printed in the USA
LVHW07*1948250618
581853LV00002B/2/P